Together in Pinecone Patch

THOMAS F. YEZERSKI

FARRAR, STRAUS AND GIROUX · NEW YORK

For Mom and Dad

Distributed in Canada by Douglas & McIntyre Ltd.
Color separations by Hong Kong Scanner Arts
Printed and bound in the United States of America by Berryville Graphics
Designed by Filomena Tuosto
First edition, 1998

Library of Congress Cataloging-in-Publication Data
Yezerski, Thomas.
    Together in Pinecone Patch / Thomas F. Yezerski. — 1st ed.
        p.   cm.
    Summary: A girl from Ireland and a boy from Poland
overcome the prejudices held by the residents of the small
American town to which they have emigrated.
    ISBN 0-374-37647-6
    [1. Prejudices—Fiction. 2. Immigrants—Fiction.
3. Love—Fiction.] I. Title.
PZ7.Y52To   1998
[E]—DC21   97-10874

IRELAND

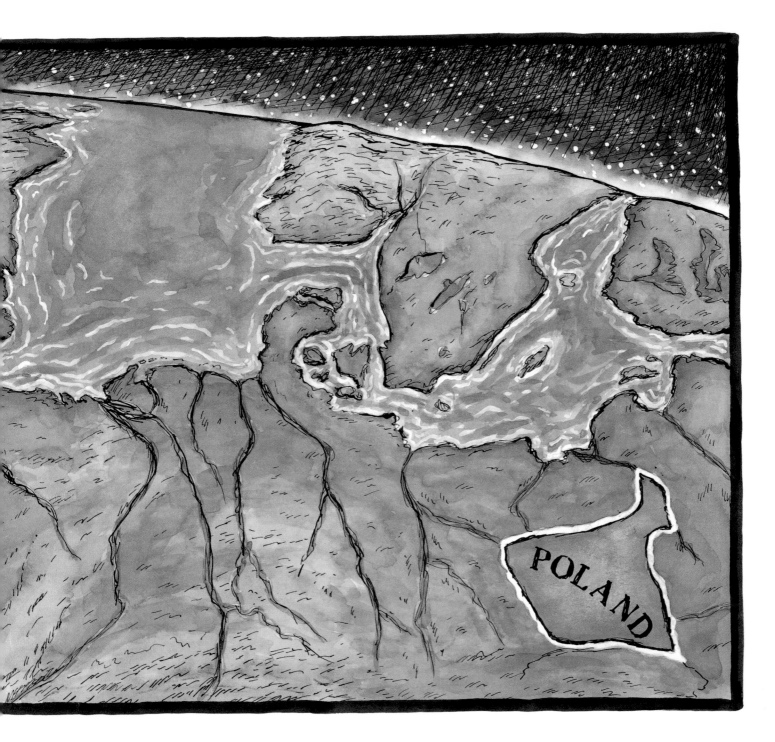

Not long ago, the people of Ireland and the people of Poland knew very little of each other. Hundreds of miles of icy seas and murky wilderness separated their countries. It seemed that all they would ever share was the stars of the night sky.

Ireland was a land covered with a blanket of gentle hills that could lull you to sleep just to look at them, if it were not for the bright green grass. It was absolutely beautiful. The people of Ireland suffered, though. The crops wouldn't come up, and there were too many people to feed.

A wide golden meadow lay across Poland, except in places where a few stubborn forests, lakes, or mountains peeked out. Poland was quite different from Ireland, but just as beautiful. Life there was hard, too. Farmers had nothing to sell, and landlords were turning them out of their rickety houses.

The Buckleys were an especially poor family in Ireland, struggling to grow potatoes on a tiny plot of land they did not even own. There were eight Buckleys in all, so there was never quite enough food. They could get rather noisy complaining about it.

The loudest voice belonged to Keara Buckley, the youngest of the six children, and the only girl. When she wasn't complaining, she liked to sing. On a clear day, her songs could be heard, note for note, from Kilkenny to Cork and back again.

Stefan Pazik was hungry, too. He lived in Poland with his father, a rye and wheat farmer. His mother had died when he was born. At night, Stefan and his father used to join Stefan's many aunts and uncles to share the strange old stories of Poland—some true and some not so much so.

Stefan was shy, but he imagined stories as enchanting as any that even his oldest aunts and uncles had ever told. There were no stories these days, though. All the talk was about the bad harvest and the coming winter.

The Buckleys decided to escape their problems in Ireland and go to America. Everyone was sad to leave Ireland and afraid of the New World. They went by boat over wide seas and by train through dark woods, packed side by side with hundreds of other fearful travelers. Even Keara's singing could not lighten the mood.

Stefan Pazik and his father also traveled to America, in the same dreadful fashion.

"How can there be a place more beautiful than Poland, or with stories more strange and wonderful?" asked Stefan.

"There is no place, my son. But in America, at least there is hope," answered Mr. Pazik.

The long, hard journey of the Buckleys and the Paziks ended on precisely the same day in precisely the same place. They were in Pinecone Patch, Pennsylvania, U.S.A.

Keara stood on West Main Street, and Stefan stood on East Main Street, looking at their new hometown. It was no Ireland and it was no Poland, but it was all they had.

Pinecone Patch was a coal-mining town. Thundering noise and black dust blew out of the giant coal breaker which towered over the town. Beneath its dirty streets, men dug coal out of the dark, wet mine. Women worked in their kitchens and tiny, crowded vegetable gardens. The people spoke many different languages, but none sounded cheerful. It was a scary place for Keara and Stefan.

There was an Irish neighborhood, and a Polish neighborhood, and each one was like a little piece of the Old Country. In the Irish neighborhood, Keara could smell her favorite food, corned beef, and hear her favorite songs. For Stefan, the Polish neighborhood had the smell of stuffed cabbage and the sound of ghost stories told late into the night.

"We'll be happy here," said Mr. Buckley to his family. "Just don't talk to those Polish people. I've heard they're a bunch of foolish good-for-nothings."

Mr. Pazik warned Stefan as well. "Be careful near the Irish neighborhood. They're all crazy rascals."

On a day when the younger children of Pinecone Patch were searching for scraps of coal near the mines, Keara Buckley and Stefan Pazik came face-to-face with each other for the first time. They froze in their tracks. Both children remembered their parents' warnings about the strangers from the other neighborhood.

It seemed to Keara that Stefan's ears were entirely too big. Stefan thought Keara's wild red hair made her look like a witch. They stared at each other, afraid to move. Finally, Keara stuck out her tongue. That was the end of the silence. Stefan dropped his pail of coal and ran off screaming.

Keara and Stefan always had chores to do, but when they were eight years old, they had to begin earning extra money for their families. Keara helped her mother sew up holes in the miners' clothes. Stefan went with his father to work at the mines. Stefan had to pass Keara's house on the way to and from work. Every time he walked past, they would yell insults at each other.

"Hey, Big Ears! Go back to Poland!" Keara would yell from her porch. It made her feel better after scrubbing the house all day. It was better than singing.

Indeed, after sorting coal all day, Stefan did not feel complete until he had shaken his fist at least once at Keara. It healed his sore fingers a lot faster than even a well-told story. "Shut up, Potato Head!" Stefan would yell, shaking his fist.

As Keara and Stefan grew up, they became the pride of their neighborhoods. Keara matured into a smart, beautiful young woman. She was a skilled seamstress who could make an old pair of trousers look like new. Stefan grew into a strong, handsome young man and an expert miner. No one could fill a coal car faster.

However, the endless hours of hard work exhausted Keara and Stefan. Eventually, the dreariness of the Pinecone Patch sky filled both their heads, and the gloominess of the mines filled both their hearts. Now, when Stefan passed Keara's house, they could no longer raise their heads to each other, let alone their fists.

One particular summer evening, when the dust was quick to settle and the sun was slow to set, Stefan passed Keara's house once more. He was so tired that he forgot where he was, and he accidentally said "Good evening" to Keara as he walked by.

Keara was so startled all she could say was "Good evening" right back to him. At the sound of Keara's sweet voice, Stefan quickly looked up. Keara looked back at him.

"Would you like to come inside for tea?" said Keara.

Stefan was surprised, of course, and said, "I can't come in. I'm tired from working all day, and I have things to do."

"Well, I myself still need to make the supper, finish the wash, bring in the firewood . . ."

"All right. I can stay a minute. It would be my pleasure," he said, and went inside.

"Why are you so friendly to me now, after all our years of bitterness?" asked Stefan, sipping his tea. "Your parents would be very angry to have a Polish man in their house."

Keara answered, "I have watched you miners pass my house for many years, and your coal-black faces are all the same, Irish or Polish. But I have watched you in particular, Stefan, and I know that behind the soot on your face is a kind and generous man."

Then she said suddenly, "Now you must go. My mother will soon return from the company store, and my father and brothers will be home from their shift at the mine. They must not see you here."

"Thank you for the tea," said Stefan. "It was delicious."

In spite of what their families might say, Keara and Stefan met secretly many other times to talk and share their troubles, which didn't seem so troublesome after a cup of tea. These meetings grew closer together, and so did Keara and Stefan. They fell so deeply in love that they no longer cared what anyone might say about seeing them together.

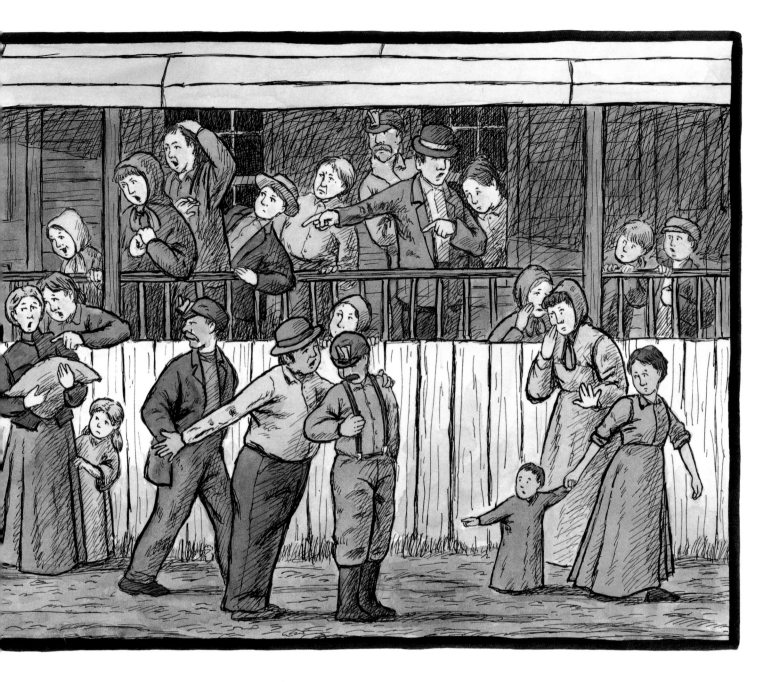

The citizens of Pinecone Patch did not look kindly on cups of tea between a Polish man and an Irish woman, but they did like to talk about it. The fences buzzed with bickering and giggling about Keara and Stefan. Soon everyone had heard the news. Some looked upon it less kindly than others.

Mrs. Buckley scolded her daughter. "Must you shame our family just for the sake of an ugly Polish miner?"

Mr. Buckley added, "What will they say, back in Ireland?"

Keara answered her parents, "Your words are just like the dreary sky, the gloomy mines, and the dirty hills around this town. My love for Stefan is higher than the clouds, deeper than the mines, and more beautiful than the gentlest hills of Ireland."

Mr. Pazik complained, "I have worked very hard to get what little we have. Why must you throw it away for a crazy Irish girl?"

Stefan told his father, "This cruel town brought Keara and me together, and it has made us strong. It cannot part us now. We are in love, and I'm going to marry her."

Mr. Pazik sighed and threw up his hands. "Well, if you're going to marry her," he said, "then we'll have to find you a nice suit."

Reluctantly, Keara's and Stefan's parents gave them their blessings. The rest of Pinecone Patch was not as quick to accept the marriage, but they all arrived on the wedding day anyway, much as they might flock to a boxing match. Surely, there would be a battle.

Keara and Stefan had a big ceremony at St. Edward's Church. It was long, too. Their parents insisted on both Irish and Polish customs. The bride and groom were so happy they didn't even notice their friends and relatives glaring at each other across the aisles of the church.

No one was sure how to celebrate after the ceremony. The Polish wanted to eat potato dumplings and dance the polka. The Irish wanted to eat potato pancakes and dance the jig. They did agree on one thing, though: they wanted to fight about it.

Just as the guests were getting their fists up, Mrs. Buckley said, "Mr. Pazik, I think I should like to learn to dance the polka."

Everyone looked at one another, surprised and confused.

Mr. Pazik turned to Mrs. Buckley and said, "I shall gladly teach you the polka, but only after you show me how to dance the jig." He held out his hand to Mrs. Buckley, and the two got up to dance.

The accordion began to play. Gradually, all of Pinecone Patch joined in the dancing of polkas and jigs. The party lasted two days. Late into the second night, Keara sang happy songs about love, and her songs could be heard from Pinecone Patch to Pottstown and back again.

Keara and Stefan lived happily together for the rest of their days. Stefan always told his children and grandchildren stories—some true and some not so much so. His favorite story was about a boy from a land of golden meadows and a girl from a land of green hills, who came thousands of miles to a town of nightmares and dreams, just to be together.